Bitty Fish

Barbara deRubertis
Illustrated by Eva Vagreti Cockrille

The Kane Press
New York

Cover Design: Sheryl Kagen

Library of Congress Catalog Card Number: 96-75013

ISBN 1-57565-002-9

10 9 8 7 6 5

First published in the United States of America in 1997 by The Kane Press.
Printed in China.

This is Bitty—
Bitty Fish.
Itty, bitty
Bitty Fish.

3

"Look," says Kim.
"I want this fish.
I want this itty
Bitty Fish."

4

"I have a dish,
a dish for fish.
This fish will fit
in my fish dish.

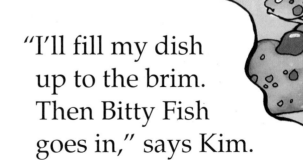

"I'll fill my dish up to the brim. Then Bitty Fish goes in," says Kim.

Bitty Fish
looks at the dish.
She does not like
the dish for fish.

"I am too BIG
to swim in this.
This is an *icky*
bitty dish.

"There are no fish
in this fish dish—
no fish friends
who swim and swish.

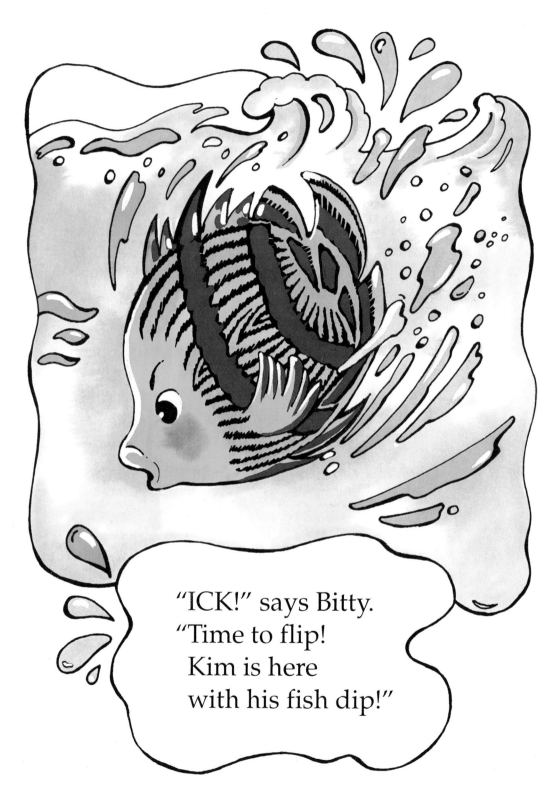

"ICK!" says Bitty.
"Time to flip!
Kim is here
with his fish dip!"

"I'll pick up Bitty Fish with this. Then I'll put her in the dish."

Look at Kim
dip and dip.
Dip, dip
for Bitty Fish.

Look at Bitty
swim and flip.
She flips her fins
to make Kim drip.

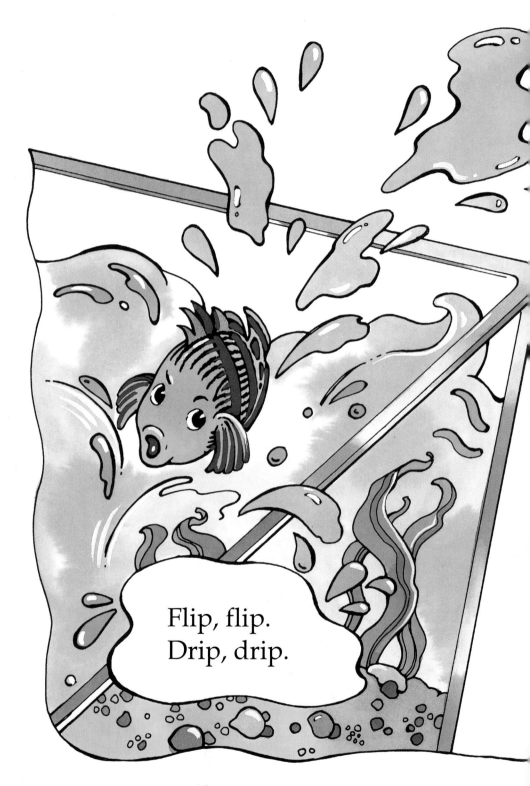

Flip, flip.
Drip, drip.

Up goes Kim.
Then Kim sits.

Bitty flips and
Bitty flits.

Now Kim grins
a silly grin.

"Bitty Fish,
you win! YOU WIN!"

Bitty grins and
grins and grins.
She wiggles with her
flippy fins.

Bitty makes a
fishy wish.
She wishes for
a bigger dish.

She wishes for
a FRIEND fish,
a friend to share
a BIG dish.

Think, Kim.
Think of wishes.
Think of what
a fish's wish is.

Kim skips
to get a dish,
a BIG dish
for TWO fish!

Then he dips
his fish dip in.

Up comes Bitty!
Up comes Trish!

Two fish friends
in one big dish!